29 Bump Street

29 Bump Street

Alain Vaës

Turner Publishing, Inc.

ATLANTA

Library of Congress Cataloging-in-Publication Data

Vaës, Alain.
    29 Bump Street/written and illustrated by Alain Vaës. —1st ed.
p. cm.
Summary: Led by an ambitious hammer named Mike, the basement tools
battle the kitchen utensils for the most desirable spot in the house.
ISBN 1-57036-292-0 (alk. paper)
[1. Tools—Fiction.   2. Kitchen utensils—Fiction.]   I. Title.
PZ7.V18Aae   1996
[E]—dc20   96-3524

                                                            CIP
                                                            AC

Published by Turner Publishing, Inc.
A Subsidiary of Turner Broadcasting System, Inc.
1050 Techwood Drive, N.W.
Atlanta, Georgia 30318

Distributed by Andrews and McMeel
A Universal Press Syndicate Company
4900 Main Street
Kansas City, Missouri 64112

First Edition 10 9 8 7 6 5 4 3 2 1
Printed in the U.S.A.

To Lydie, Celine, and Thibault.

Down in
the dark,
dreary
basement
of 29 Bump
Street, the house tools
were hanging out and feeling restless again.

"I haven't used my head in months,"
sighed Mike Hammer as he scratched
his claw against a wooden box.

"Hey, Walter Wrench," said Penny Plane,
"remember the time you fixed that
drippy faucet?"

"Yep, I really had a grip back then,"
Walter replied.

"Twister," murmured Flathead Screwdriver
to his sister, "we sure turned a lot of heads
in the kitchen, didn't we?"

The tools' lives were filled with daydreams of busy times upstairs. And every night, they drifted off to sleep while listening to Sammy Saw bend his blade and sing "The Cool Tool Blues."

That night Mike Hammer felt edgy, remembering his favorite job, which was hanging pictures in the kitchen.

"Ahh," Mike sighed. "What a fun place. Those kitchen folks have all the luck. They bake, fry, slice, and mix while we just sit and rust."

"It's not fair," Vinny Vise agreed, letting out a loud yawn that woke the entire Nails family. "But what can we do?"

"Heck, I bet *we* could run the kitchen!" hammered Mike.

But the kitchen had changed
a lot since the last time the tools visited . . .

The Silverware popped out of their drawer
and looked around. "Well, friends," Nicky Knife
complained, "this place is *still* a wreck!"

Calvin Coffeepot agreed. He looked at the
other members of the kitchen family and
felt terrible. "If we don't do something soon,
this will be a disaster area!"

Sure enough, things got worse...

"We all need a good scrubbing," bubbled Peggy Pot, "but I'm not going to jump into that slime!"

"Give me a break," mumbled Mickey Mug. "With the sink clogged, we're going to stick around in this gunk for a long time."

"Talk about tarnishing my image!" forked Freddy.

Whack!

Molly Meat Mallet decided to play her favorite game, "Pulverize the Fly."

Blake Blender, Jenn Cookie Jar, Suzie Seltzer Bottle, and Calvin were sizing up the kitchen trash.

"Can you believe those knuckleheads?" Calvin asked, pointing to some utensils who were depleting the fishbowl.

Calvin took a deep breath and poured out his feelings. "It's time for a change!" he announced. "We *have* to straighten up this kitchen!"

And as the kitchen clan made their plans, something
began brewing downstairs . . .

"It's really time for a change," Mike pounded away.
"We're bored, and we deserve a better life!"

Vinny Vise unclamped his jaw. "I'm with you, Mike!

C'mon everyone!

Let's repair—I mean *prepare* to go upstairs!"

In a blur of rusty metal and dusty wood, the tools clanged up the stairs, chanting, "Let's climb to the top!"

The kitchen bunch heard all the racket and crowded up at the basement door, not knowing what was about to happen.

Tap, Tap, Tap, Tap

Bang, Bang, Bang

The door burst open and in went the tool gang.

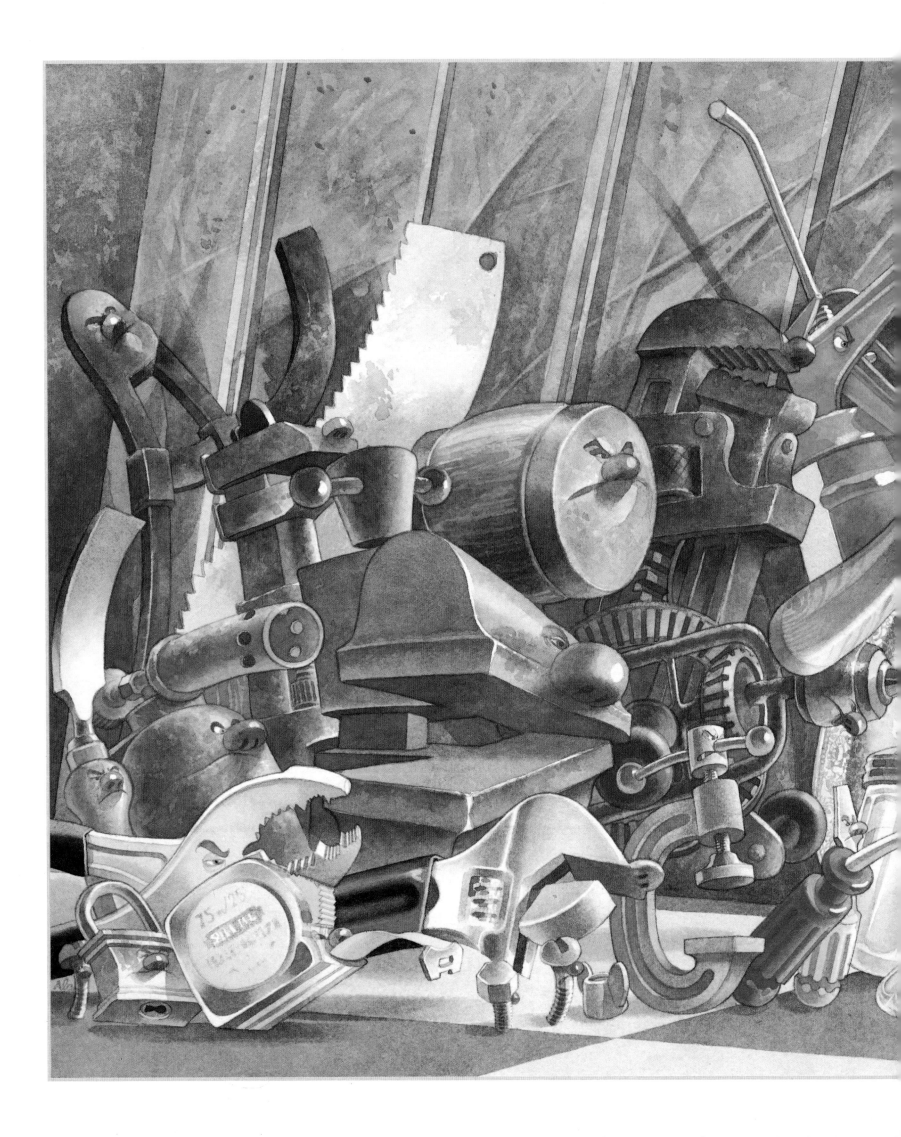

The kitchen at 29 Bump Street became an awful sight . . .

"We want the good life!" sparked Benny Blowtorch. Then he French roasted Gary Grinder.

The toast went flying when Mike zonked T. J.'s stainless top.

A few dishes got cracked, and some forks were bent.

Calvin waved a dishcloth in the air.

"Stop! We give up!"

25

Mike Hammer stepped forward. "We want the kitchen!"

"That's right," Linda Lantern snickered. "It's our turn to live in the light."

As the kitchen family shuffled down the basement steps, the tools looked around for what to do next.

"I know!" suggested Mike.

"Let's make lunch!"

"Charge!" whirled Denny Drill as he poked a green pepper.

"Lett-us fix something to eat," Sheila Shears giggled.

The tools were having a blast...

"This kitchen stuff is very a-peeling," whittled Penny Plane.

Mike tapped too hard on the eggs and they eggs-ploded. Egg shells and egg yolks went everywhere.

"HA, HA!" Vinny Vise broke up.

"Making lunch is not what it's cracked up to be," Mike mumbled.

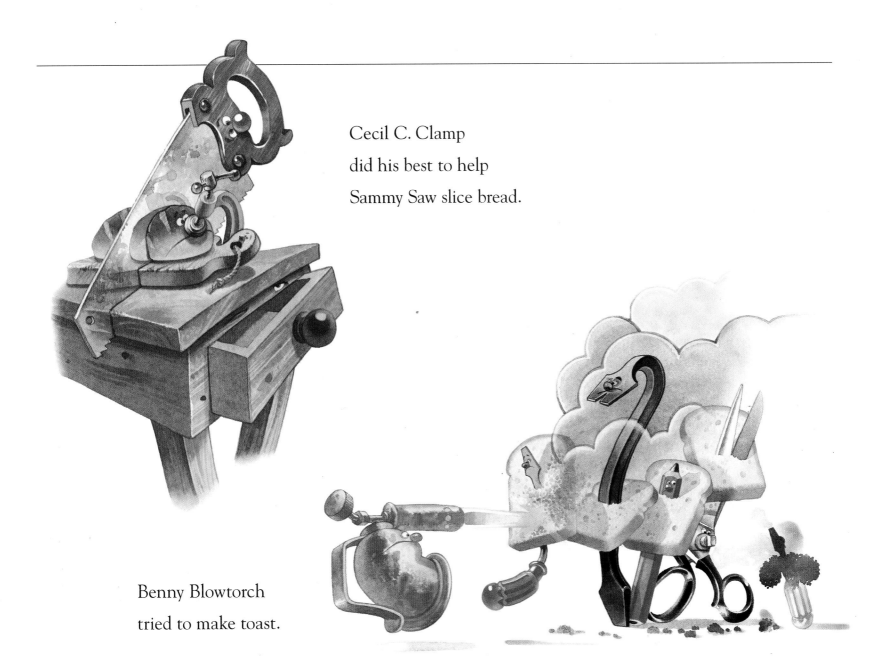

Cecil C. Clamp
did his best to help
Sammy Saw slice bread.

Benny Blowtorch
tried to make toast.

Mike Hammer and
Vinny Vise (giving
up on egg cracking)
attempted to make
orange juice.

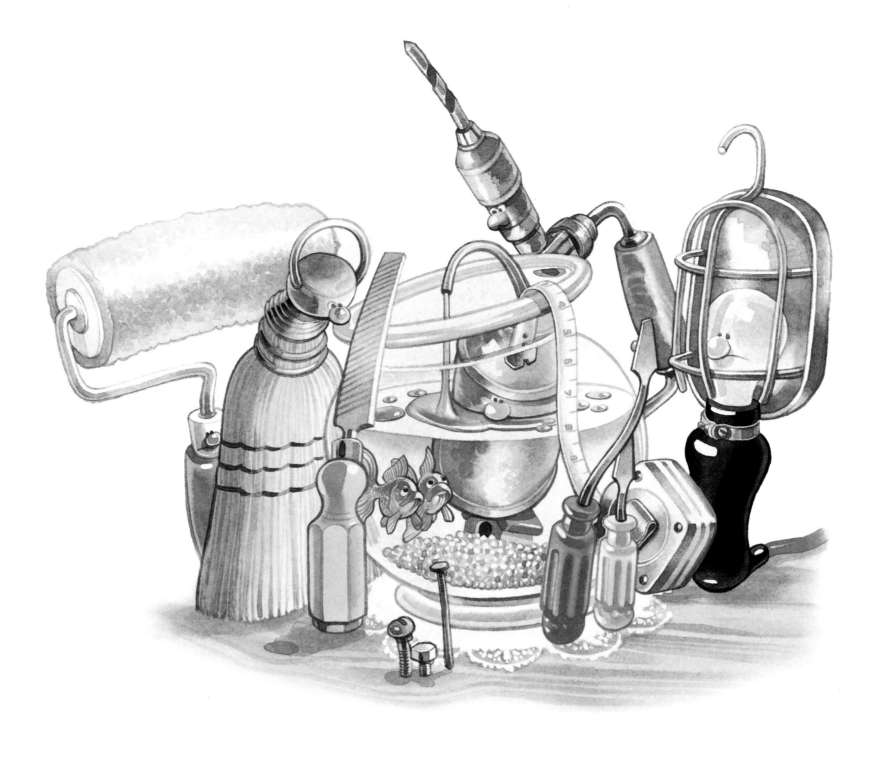

Across the room, Oliver Oilcan was sitting on the edge of the fishbowl, trying to catch a fish for lunch. Suddenly, he slipped.

Glug, glug, glug.

"Hey, that's not too slick," Flathead whispered to Twister. "Oil and water don't mix!" Things were not going swimmingly in the kitchen.

"That was some meal we made," said Sammy Saw, "but I'm all bent out of shape, and my teeth hurt. Maybe we shouldn't have cut those flowers for the salad."

"All *I* made," declared Mike, "was a mess!"

"What are we going to do?" cried Walter Wrench, clenching up in fear of rusting.

The tools gathered around in gloom, and Sammy began to croon.

"We need help,"

thought Mike, as he tried to get the sticky goop off his nose.

Meanwhile in the basement...

Calvin Coffeepot nudged Egbert Eggbeater, who looked particularly sad. "We could brighten up this place. After all, we were going to clean the kitchen anyway."

After some discussion, each member of the kitchen family started doing things they had never tried before.

"Steady, Blake!" flipped Pat Spatula, as she, Blake Blender, and Suzie teamed up to wash the walls.

Freddy Fork scraped the grime from the floor, while Egbert whirled the dirt into a pile.

"Heavenly," sighed Sandy Sponge as she soaked up the bubbly hot water. "I'm ready for a good rubdown."

Calvin Coffeepot proudly announced, "We're baking—I mean *making* the basement a better place."

But upstairs...

Mike was feeling steel blue. He decided to hit the road to find help and remembered the fine, fancy folks in the dining room.

He leaned his head against the dining room door until it swung open.

"Hello?" Mike stammered.

"It's Mr. Hammer," Sterling T. Service formally announced.

Several members of other families of 29 Bump Street had huddled together in the dining room, expecting the tools to come rushing in at any moment.

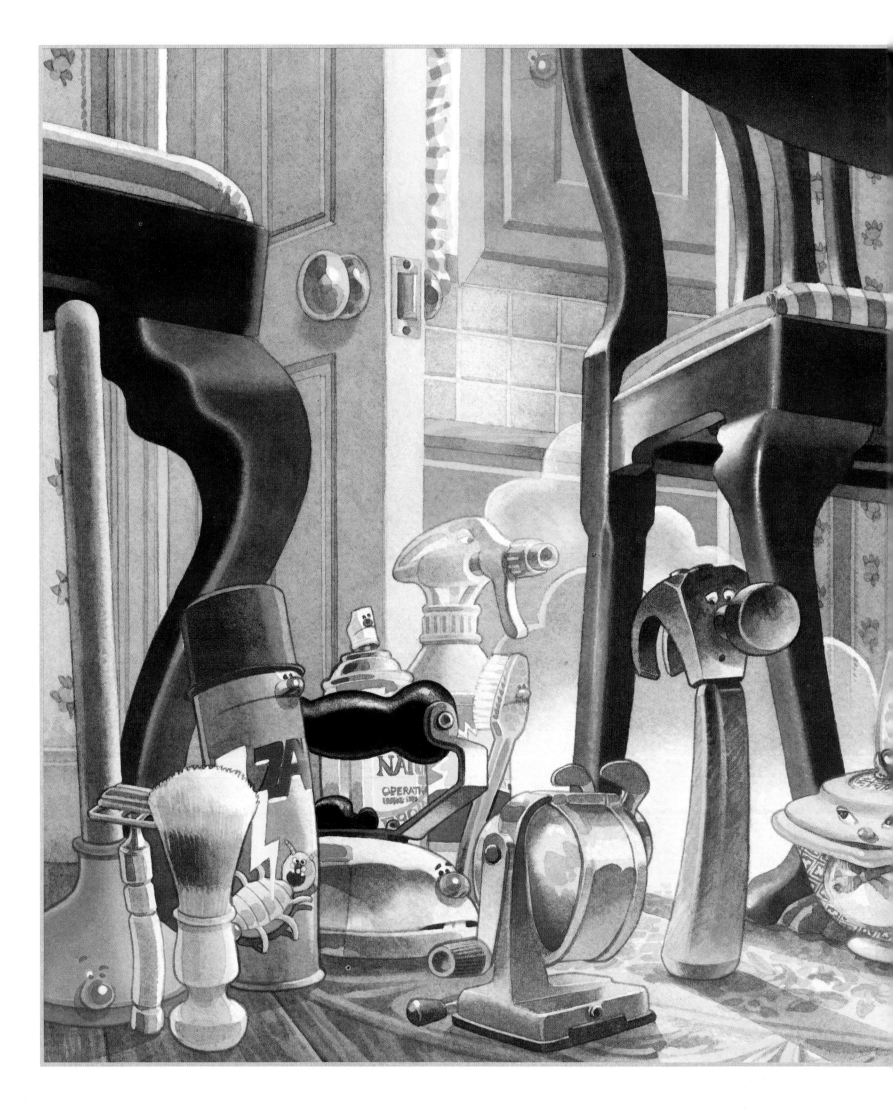

Sarah Sugar Bowl tried to smile and be friendly.

"What can we do for you, Sweetie?"

"I'm afraid we've made a terrible mistake!" said Mike. "We were bored with the basement, but we've made a mess in the kitchen."

Mike's head was feeling very heavy, but he continued. "We even kicked Calvin and the others out of their home. Sugar, what do you think we should do?"

Sarah's voice was crystal clear.

"I remember the sweet old days at 29 Bump Street when the tools kept the place in tip-top shape. In fact, we all pitched in and helped one another."

She paused, then said, "This poor house needs a lot of work. Old Trevor Trunk told us the attic needs fixing and cleaning; there's a hole in the roof, and . . ."

"Go talk to your friends, Mike," pleaded Sarah.

Mike had a new handle on life.

"Tools," Mike hammered away with new enthusiasm, "we are all very good at doing certain tasks. But as we have all discovered, there are some things that we need others for."

The tools looked around the wrecked kitchen and nodded in agreement.

"Remember how we tools *used* to take care of 29 Bump Street?" Mike asked.

Some of the tools started to smile.

"We're with you, Mike!" hollered Flathead and Twister. "But we will need the kitchen family's help."

"Great!" thumped Mike. "Let's go get everyone together."

"Hooray!"

burst Darla Doorknob as she swung open the basement door. The tools marched happily down the stairs.

"This is awesome!"

Mike cried out. "The basement looks terrific."

"How did the kitchen family do all of this?" asked Sammy Saw.

"It's beautiful!" the tools exclaimed.

Vinny's steel mouth was the first to drop open. "I'm afraid we didn't do as well in the kitchen," he confessed.

Mike quickly spoke up. "Listen, we've been thinking. We live in the same house, and we gizmos should all work together. Please come back upstairs, and we'll all put things right."

"Mike, you've hit the nail right on the head!" expressed Calvin.

And with that,

they set to work, making their world
a better place—handle in handle.

The author would like to thank the following
for helping to shape this book . . .

Jane Lahr, Star Reese, Ben Aronson, Alan Axelrod,
Walton Rawls, Michael Reagan, and Michael Walsh.

Editor: Dee Ann Grand
Copy Chief: Lauren Emerson
Design: Carol Norton
Production: Anne Murdoch
Title Treatment: James L. Lebbad
Color Separations: PrintNet
Printer: Horowitz-Rae